Mephistopheles meets his match

Aurthor:

Doris Smith

To my Children, Grandchildren, and Great-Grandchildren this book is lovingly dedicated. Though I may one day depart, the stories that have captured your hearts and imaginations will endure, carrying on for generatioms. I Cherish each and every one of you dearly.

Love Mom / Dee Dee

MEPHISTOPHELES MEETS HIS MATCH

"Kris", shouted Mrs. Conway. "Get down

this instant or...Oh no!" Mrs. Conway ran to

the tree where Kris now lay, clothing torn

and covered with mud, her hair full of

leaves and scratches evident on all

uncovered portions of her body.

"My foot, it hurts", moaned Kris.

Much later, after Dr. Saunders had departed, Mrs. Conway entered Kris' room. Kris, lying in bed in a fresh nightgown, looking much subdued, bore little resemblance to the 13-year-old of just a short hour previous.

"Why Kris? Why do you do such things? Why do you have to behave in such a reckless manner? Even your name. Insisting everyone call you Kris and refusing to answer if they do not. And you have such a lovely name, Kristabel.

I don't know what I'm going to do with

you...what on earth were you doing half

way up that tree?"

"Aw, mama, Bobby, Susie and Katie was..."

began Kris.

"Robert, Suzanne and Katrina were",

corrected Mrs. Conway.

"Yes'm. Robert, Suzanne and Katrina was

talkin' and..."

"Were talking."

"Were talking...mama, how can I tell you if

you keep interrupting me?"

"Very well, tell it your own way."

"Well, they was...er...were talking and we

got to cutting up and one thing led to

another and then they said no one could

climb to the top of the ole Oak, *n I said I

could, 'n they bet I couldn't and then they dared me and..."

"And naturally you had to take the dare...Oh, Kristabel, I swear you'll either kill yourself one day, or kill me in the attempt. For twins you and Katrina are as unlike as night is to day."

"It wasn't the dare, mama, it was the bet. They each bet me fifty cents 'gainst the silver dollar Gramps give me and that would have been a dollar and a half I'd win..."

"Which you didn't."

"No, ma'am", murmured Kris in a small voice, "I lost."

"You always lose," taunted Katrina who had just entered the room.

"Do not!"

"Do, too!"

"I do not and you just shut up Katie Conway or when I get up, you'll wish you had", threatened Kris.

"Sez you. You always take a dare but you never win the bet. You couldn't win if your middle name was win."

Kris grabbed for Katie who easily danced out of her sister's range.

"Girls! Girls! Stop this instant! Katrina leave the room."

"Yes'm", said Katie. After Katie departed, Mrs. Conway turned to Kris.

"Kristabel, what is it that drives you to do such stupid, dangerous stunts? Like the time you broke your arm walking that fence, or slid down from the barn roof into the haystack and punctured your leg on the rake? Thank heavens it was only your leg. It could have easily been your eye, or you could have missed the hay entirely and broke your neck. You've broken just about every bone in your body at some time or other. Today it's only a sprained ankle but who knows what it's going to be tomorrow or the next day at the rate you're going. It's time you grew up. Tomorrow is your fourteenth birthday and starting tomorrow you're going to act like a young lady...and dress like one. No more pants! AND, no more bets or dares. I mean this Kristabel."

"But mama, if they bet me or dare me and I don't take it, they'll think I'm chicken."

"Well, I'd rather have a live chicken than a dead daredevil for a daughter."

"But, mama..."

"No, Kristabel. This time I really do mean what I say. Furthermore, I want you to promise me you'll do what I say. If you don't, I'll speak to your father and you won't get that horse he promised for your birthday. I mean it, Kristabel."

From her mother's tone of voice, Kris knew it was no use to argue. Her mother meant business. So, she meekly agreed, "I promise."

Mrs. Conway knew that the same strange code of behavior which prompted her daughter to always take a bet or dare was

also one, because of her

daughter's character - a curious mixture of

angel and imp - which would preclude

breaking her word once given. Mrs. Conway

felt she had just won a major victory. She

relented a little.

"I'll tell you what, Kris. I'll meet you half

way. Promise you won't take a bet or dare

for one year, and see if I'm not right. By that

time, I'm hoping

you'll be sufficiently grown up to realize that

all those stunts were childish and

dangerous."

"O.K. mama, It's a deal."

The next morning, Kris and Katie woke bright and early. It was their birthday! Katie dressed quickly and raced out to the stables, while Kris had to

practice patience (which was not one of her virtues) until her mother could assist her to the stables.

On arriving at the stables, Kris forgot her sprained ankle on seeing the two beautiful Chestnut Bays.

"This one's mine", declared Katie, "and her name is Tawny".

Kris was elated. It was the other animal who

had captured her attention. There was a

certain look in the mare's eye, a certain way

she moved her head

that made Kris feel immediately that they

were kindred spirits. Playing it cool, Kris

replied, "The only reason you got first pick is because I sprained my ankle.

Oh well, okay, I'll take this one. I think I'll call her Lucky."

"Lucky! Why that sounds like a boy's name", taunted Katie.

"Um.m.m..maybe you're right. I know! I'll call her Lucky Lady!"

"I bet you a quarter mine's faster than yours."

"I bet...", just in time Kris remembered her promise to her mother.

"Well, I know Lucky Lady can beat yours any day of the week, but I can't race you because of my ankle."

"Ha! Some excuse. You just know you'll lose and that's why you won't bet. Or maybe you're scared of falling off. I dare you! I double dare you!"

Kris, while inwardly seething, ignored Katie's taunts and refused to answer. After realizing she was not getting any reaction from her twin, Katie turned and led Tawny out of the stables.

Time passed, and after two or three months, Katie's interest in Tawny diminished. Except for occasional morning or evening rides, she more or less forgot about the mare, leaving her care to her father's stable hands. Not so Kris, she brushed and combed and curried Lucky Lady until she shone. She exercised her faithfully and spent every moment she could with her. She taught her tricks and as time passed, the rapport between animal and human increased, forging a deep bond of affection.

"I do declare", Mrs. Conway remarked one morning to her husband. "It seems Kristabel spends every waking hour with that animal.

She ought to spend

more time with boys and girls her age like

Katrina. I should have planned a party

tomorrow for their fifteenth birthday.

Maybe it's still not too late. But I

must say Kristabel has changed. She's not as

helter-skelter as she used to be, so probably

I owe that horse a vote of thanks."

At that moment, Kris had just returned from

her evening ride. She was convinced that

Lucky Lady was the smartest animal alive

and certain she understood everything said

to her, "In just one more day", Kris was

telling Lucky Lady, "I'll be fifteen. I wonder

what mama and daddy are going to give

me. Well, whatever it is, I just know I'll

never get another birthday present as

wonderful as you. Why I bet with you being

so smart and with the tricks I've taught you

we could become famous...I bet..." Kris

stopped. The thought had just struck her,

exactly one year ago, today she had

promised her mother not to take any bets

or dares for a year and today the time was

up! She could take all the bets and dares

she wanted.

"Funny, I just thought of it. And you know something, Lady? It hasn't bothered me at all - but then I've got you to thank for that. Really. Since I've had you, I haven't been spending as much time with those goofs who are always bettin' or darin', Besides, it is foolish to take a bet or dare if you don't know you can win. Or at least think you've a chance at winning. I guess mama was right. I am growing up." At this time, Kris dropped the curry comb and stooped to pick it up.

"But suppose you could always win?"

"Well, that would be different, then I'd...",

Kris straightened up quickly.

There wasn't a single soul in sight.

"Who...who said that?"

"I did, that's who."

Kris thought she must have had too much

sun. It sounded like those words were

coming from Lucky Lady. She knew she was

smart, but not that smart! Kris walked

closer to Lucky Lady and holding her jaws

tried peering into her mouth.

"Did you speak to me?"

"Yes. I spoke to you." The words were

definitely coming from Lucky Lady's mouth,

but Kris was holding her jaws and they

weren't moving.

"Why haven't you spoken to me before, Lady?"

"Because she can't speak, that's why. This is me."

"Well, who are you and where are you?"

"Right here I am and if you'll just hold Lady's mouth open a little wider...that's it." All of a sudden there was a swoosh and then standing before Kris was a man wearing a suit with wide shoulders, pointed shoes, and twirling a chain, the other end of which dangled from his front pant pocket.

Kris had never before seen the likes of this

sort of clothing.

"Where did you come from and what kind

of clothes are those? "

"Oh, is this not the attire of the era? This is what's called a zoot suit, m'dear. But I'd better change to something more conventional." So, saying he snapped his fingers and immediately his clothing changed to a double-breasted suit, with spats, straw hat and cane. Kris giggled. The man, looking somewhat annoyed, studied Kris' attire then snapped his fingers once more. This change attired him in jeans and a flannel shirt. Nodding, as if pleased with himself, he turned to Kris.

"You're not the least bit afraid of me, are you?"

"No, should I be?"

"Not at all, m'dear, not at all."

"You haven't answered me. How did you get in Lady's mouth?"

"Well, let's just say that's a trade secret."

"Well, never mind how you got there, if you really were in there, but why were you in there in the first place?"

"Self-preservation m'dear, I was attempting to avoid an old enemy and took refuge in your horse's mouth in sheer desperation."

All the events leading up to this time had occurred so quickly that Kris hadn't had time to be afraid, but now that

the shock and surprise were wearing off,

she was becoming uneasy. The stranger, as

if sensing this, said quickly,

"Now, as for what I am doing here, it's like I

said earlier, how would you like to always

win a bet, or dare?"

"I'd like that. Who wouldn't? But how can

I?"

"Well, I could arrange it."

"What's the catch?"

"That's the trouble with you younger

generation. Always looking for a catch.

Always suspicious. Well, there is a small fee,

but I don't expect to collect now. Oh, no. If

you'll just sign a contract agreeing to pay a

certain fee to me after a certain time has

expired, you'll be able to win every bet you

make."

"What is that small fee?"

"Why m'dear, don't you trust me?"

"No."

"That's certainly blunt enough. Well,

m'dear, there is a catch. You don't learn the

fee until I come back to collect it in...well,

let's say 5 years...that's fair, isn't it? Just

think of all the bets you could win in five

years. You could become the richest person

in the world. How about it?"

"I'm thinking,. Not of the bets...I'm thinking

you're the devil and you want my soul."

"Why would you think that? Simply because

I can do a few parlor tricks..."

"Well, then, what is your name and who are

you?"

"You may call me Mr. Mephistopheles,"

"Just what I thought. You're the devil and

you want my soul." Kris' seeming bravado

was only a facade. Inside she was terrified

but she was determined not to show it.

"Oh. You've heard the name. You're one of

the bright ones. Yes, my dear, I am who you

say...the devil...but I'd much prefer being

called Mr. Mephistopheles. Much more

dignified, you know. But what on earth

makes you think I want your soul? I have

much more of that commodity than I want.

No. That's not the price. You have my word

on it. I can assure you, too, that the

reputation I have acquired is due to persons

I have outwitted. I never go back on the

exact letter of my word. I might try to dupe

someone by letting them think what I say

means something else - or promise

something with a loophole in it to get what I

want, but I have always delivered and

fulfilled what I promised exactly.

It's just that men are such fools and what

they want and the way they ask for it are

two different things entirely. I take

advantage of this. I admit it. But my dear

girl, I never go back on my word. I'll tell you

what. You're a bright girl. I'll let you word

the agreement to your liking and, if at the

end of the five years when I come to collect,

if you don't like the price, we'll cancel the

deal. Now, you can't get much better than

that. How about it?"

"There's got to be some catch, though, there's got to be one."

"Can you find one?"

"Not right now, but I will if I think long enough."

"Come, come. I have other business elsewhere and I must have an answer now."

"And I get to draw up the agreement?"

"Yes. Here is paper and pen," said the devil as he materialized the needed items from apparently nothing.

"No blood?"

"Oh, that's foolishness. That was strictly for show in medieval times. It was what people expected. But come, m'dear. You're wasting time."

Kris thought for a few minutes, then, taking pen in hand, wrote the following:

I, Satan, also known as the devil,

Beelzebub, Mr.

Mephistopheles and various other

nomenclatures, do solemnly promise from

this moment on August 5, 1965, at 5:45

p.m., to grant Kristable Conway, known

also as Kris Conway, the ability

to win every bet or dare she makes, or is

made to her, no matter what it involves, no

matter how. ridiculous, difficult, silly or

seemingly impossible and no matter what

the circumstances, and further vow that

she nor any other person, animal, or thing,

living, dead or inanimate, will be hurt in

any way, shape or form as a result or

consequence of the bet or dare involved.

Further, if I, Satan, fail to allow Kristabel

Conway to win each and every bet or dare

up to the exact moment of payment, five

years hence, at 5:45 p.m., August 5, 1970,

this will render this contract

null and void, and in such instance, will

allow Kristabel Conway to retain all profits,

material and immaterial, which were

achieved or received as a

result of winning a bet or dare, and at the

same time allow her to forego paying the

price of this agreement, whatever it shall

be.

Further, if the price is not agreeable to

Kristabel Conway, this contract may be

cancelled by her, however, in such event

she will forfeit the right to retain all

benefits accrued as a result of said

agreement.

Further, that payment cannot be collected

until five years exactly have passed, i.e.,

August 5, 1970 at 5:45 pm, and Kristabel

Conway has the right to make and win bets

up until that exact moment. No payment

may be demanded without physical

presentation of this document at the

agreed-on time of August 5, 1970 at 5:45

pm.

Leaving a space for the signatures of both

parties, Kris then wrote at the bottom of the

document...

I, Kristabel Conway, agree on this date,

August 5, 1965, to pay the price demanded

in according to the above agreement, on

presentation of this document, provided

the terms of said contract are adhered to

exactly as written heretofore.

Again, she left spaces for both signatures

and handed the document to Mr.

Mephistopheles to read.

"Well, your written verbiage certainly

reflects more maturity than your spoken

word", observed the devil.

"English composition is my favorite subject",

advised Kris.

"It seems you've thought of everything. But,

I want one thing added.

You cannot bet I will allow you to keep

whatever the price I quote at the end of the

five years." Kris agreed to this and added it

to the contract. The devil then quickly

signed, dated the document and handed it to Kris who did the same. Satan then pulled the contract back so quickly that Kris had a moment of doubt.

"Now then, I'll just take this agreement with me for safekeeping, you might lose it or something else might accidentally happen to it and we wouldn't want that, would we?" Then just as suddenly as he appeared, he was gone, leaving only an echo of the most sinister laugh Kris had ever heard.

Kris stood silently for a moment. Had all that really happened? It all seemed so unreal.

At this moment, Katie, Susie, Bobby and a couple of other friends rounded the stable.

"Oh, there you are Kris", said Katie sweetly... much too sweetly. "I was just telling the kids about all the tricks you've taught Lucky Lady and all the stunts you can do. They don't believe me. I told them you were so good I bet you could even stand on your head and ride her, they bet you couldn't...but I forgot...you don't take bets or dares any longer."

"Oh, I don't know. If it was worth my while I might. How about that silver bracelet you have that I like. Want to bet that?"

Katie, taken aback at Kris' complete turnaround over what she had come to expect during the past year stammered, "Well, er,..all right."

"Okay, then", and so saying Kris mounted Lucky Lady.

Katie, now frightened at this turn of events because she didn't really want anything to happen to Kris cried, "Kris, you can't stand on your head and ride her, Get down! I was only trying to get your goat. Please! I was only kidding. You can have the bracelet. Please, please get down!"

"Well, I wasn't kidding. I meant it and I bet you I can do it, too." With that statement Kris proceeded to stand on her head on Lucky Lady and commanded her to trot in a circle.

Katie and the others were stunned, but no one more than Kris. I can do it. I really can.

It wasn't a dream. It really happened. Boy oh boy, just wait! Will I have fun now!

From that day forward good fortune continuously smiled on Kris. She won all bets, no matter the seemingly impossible odds. However, Kris did not revert back to the mischievous, in-trouble-every-minute youngster of previous years. She had grown up!

Kris' family also reaped the benefits of her good fortune. When her father was facing financial ruin and the loss of his business Kris came to his rescue with "Don't worry father, I bet something good will happen soon" and, sure enough, that very next day

an old friend came to the house to repay Mr.

Conway for his kindness in investing a large

sum of money in the friend's faltering

business. The business venture had paid off

handsomely and the return on Mr. Conway's

investment was such a staggering amount

that he was able to repay all debts and

reestablish himself as a well to do

businessman.

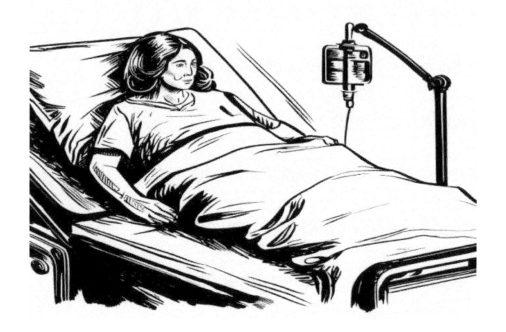

When Mrs. Conway suffered a heart attack

and the doctors did not think she would pull

through, Kris assured her family, "She'll be

all right, I just know she will. Why I bet

tomorrow she'll be like her old self." Sure

enough, to the astonishment of her doctors,

Mrs. Conway made an amazing recovery.

Through the years Kris was responsible for saving a friend from being gored by a steer, saved her sister from having her eye put out by a wild arrow and many other incidents of similar nature. As time passed, Kris became a beautiful young woman, wealthy in her own right. By picking a stock at random and investing some money left to her by her grandmother, then betting it would go way up, she started on the road to her first million,

Through all of her good fortune, Kris still found time to spend with Lucky Lady.

By this time Lady had become famous,

winning race after race since the first time

Kris had entered her and bet her to win. The

affection between Lady and Kris was a

wonderful thing.

One evening, after a particularly tiring day,

Kris retired to her room to rest before

getting ready to go out for the evening. Her

fiancé was taking her and her family to

dinner and a show to celebrate her birthday.

She had just taken off her shoes and was

about to remove her clothes when...

"Good evening, m'dear",

Kris wheeled around. There, standing before

her, looking almost exactly as he had looked

that day of their first encounter, was Mr.

Mephistopheles.

"Why, what are you doing here?" Even as

she said it, Kris remembered.

"Today, it's five years exactly today, isn't it?"

"That's right, today is August 5, 1970, your

twentieth birthday, and five years to the

date we made our agreement. As you see,

I've brought it with me and come to collect

payment."

"Very well. Tell me what it is so I may pay

you and then you can go."

"Not a very cordial welcome m'dear. And

after all I've done for you."

"Look, I'm expecting a guest and I'd like to get some rest before I go out for the evening."

"A guest...now isn't that nice. Mr. Rory Stanton. I'd say he was more than just a guest, wouldn't you?"

"Never mind. I just don't want you around when he comes."

"You're rather ungrateful, you know."

"All right. All right. We have an agreement. Tell me the price and then go."

"Very well, m'dear. The price is Lucky Lady."

"Kris exploded. "Lucky Lady! Never! Never in a million years! **No, no, no**"

"Oh but yes, yes, yes. I kept my end of the bargain. Now you keep yours."

"No! I won't! I'll give you a million dollars, I'll give..."

"Now what would I do with your million dollars? I can get anything I want. Some things are harder than others and that is why I make deals. Right now, I'm collecting one. I want Lucky Lady."

"But why? There must be something else. There must be! Why do you want Lucky Lady?"

"Call it a whim. Say it's a because she's such a beautiful, smart animal.

Say it's because she provided me refuge from my enemy. Nevertheless, I mean to have her. No, m'dear. There is nothing else. I want her. I've kept my word, now you keep yours."

"Wait, the agreement says if I don't agree on the price, I can cancel the agreement."

"True. You may do that, but then you'll forfeit your right to all things obtained as a result of the agreement."

"I don't care. Take everything. I'll have enough money to get by. Not all my money is a result of a bet. And Lucky Lady is fast. I timed her before I entered and bet her to win. She can still win races. Besides..."

"Besides..." interrupted the devil, "you're planning to get married soon and money doesn't mean much to you anyway, does it? You use your money to help others. I know of all your charities and good deeds. But I wasn't only referring to material goods when I said you would forfeit everything. I was referring to other things also."

"What other things?"

"Your mother's health, for instance."

"What has my mother's health to do with this?"

"Didn't you bet your mother would recover from a heart attack when everyone was certain she would die? And what about your father? Didn't your betting save him from financial ruin? And your sister's eyesight? and fiancé.

Didn't he just recently survive a train wreck, the only survivor from that particular car I might add. And Lucky Lady herself! If you cancel the agreement, you won't have her anyway. You pulled her through by betting the veterinarian you could succeed when he gave up. So, you see, m'dear. You have no choice. It's Lucky Lady, OR, Lucky Lady, your fiancé, your family and everything else."

Kris was despaired and, at the same time, frantic and angry at having made such a neat trap for herself. She raved, yelled, cried and pleaded. To no avail. She knew the devil had won and wanted, more than anything, to slap that smirk off of his face. But that wouldn't change things. He had won, fair and square. Or...had he? Kris fought for control. There was a glimmer of an idea percolating

in back of her mind. She must think.

"Well, it seems you've won. But wait. It's just 5:39 p.m. By the terms of the agreement, I have six more minutes. The agreement states you cannot collect until the exact time is up."

"Why prolong the agony? Get it over with!"

"No! The agreement also states I have a right to bet up until that moment and if you fail to let me win then the contract is null and void and I get to keep everything."

"Very well, m'dear. If you are going to quibble. But what could you possibly hope to gain by it?"

"Never mind, can I still bet?"

"Yes, yes. Get it over with."

"Very well. Here is the bet. I bet you that contract you are holding doesn't exist."

It took a few moments for her words to sink in...and then...Satan was sputtering and fuming..."You can't do that! I won't allow it! I WILL NOT ALLOW IT!"

"Very well, if you don't then you aren't living up to the words of the contract by allowing me to win each and every bet so then the contract is null and void and I am allowed to keep everything without payment."

"But", shouted Satan. "If I do let you win the bet and this contract doesn't exist, I still can't collect. This contract must be presented at the time of payment! How can I collect with a contract that doesn't exist? If I let you win the bet, I lose. And if I don't let you win the bet, I still lose!!!"

"You might say you can't win for losing," crowed Kris.

"You...you...not since Daniel Webster has this happened to me...you...you!" Satan was infuriated with rage. He was sputtering incoherently. He swished his hand. A sudden burst of fire encompassed him.

Another swish, Then! Satan, flames and

contract were gone!

Tears rolled down Kris' cheeks as her tightly

strung nerves relaxed, relieved of the terror

and panic of the last few moments. She

breathed a sigh of relief. She had learned

her lesson. And learned it well! Never again!

It would be a cold day in hell before she ever

again bet on anything!

Kris whispered a little prayer for her

deliverance. She knew she had been very

lucky. The old saying about no one getting

something for nothing could

very well have proven true.

And, there is a moral to this story,.. DON'T

LOOK A GIFT HORSE IN THE MOUTH.

Milton Keynes UK
Ingram Content Group UK Ltd.
UKHW051117140823
426838UK00014B/696